® Ella & Ellie LLC.

This book is dedicated to Ella's father, Dale,

who taught her that if she loves something, give it her all.

There are so many individuals we would like to thank. This book took a collective mix of people and we are extremely grateful for the support. In no particular order:

To Elle's family, including her mother, father, and three younger sisters.

To Ella's family, especially her mother and three brothers, for always believing in Ella and Elle as they pursued this endeavor.

To Jim Dunlap, without you Ella and Elle wouldn't have been able to make this happen. Thank you for your guidance.

To Ellen Wall, thank you for proofing various copies of the manuscript and all of Ella's important college papers. You are an amazing friend.

To Daniel, thank you for being the greatest partner to Ella through the processes of writing this book and throughout her days. Your unyielding pride and support is forever appreciated.

To the family that inspired this story, words will never be able to explain how important you are to Ella. Thank you.

To God, thank you for blessing Ella and Elle with the ability and opportunity to make this idea a reality.

Mommy and Daddy

love you so...

yet, off to work

they must go.

They searched for someone
to fill their shoes.

Not just anyone
could they choose.

After a while they found me,

and your nanny I came to be.

Little did I know; I had not a clue...

Each day with you would bring something new!

we shared moments of laughter.

you made my days brighter.

from time to time I heard you cry.

More often than not,

it seemed you could fly.

I watched you grow,

and I want you to know:

Even when we are
apart,

you are always in
my heart.

About the Author

Ella D. grew up in Southeastern Wisconsin. After earning her Bachelor of Arts and Communications in Journalism, she ventured off into the world as a young, eager professional...who had no clue what she wanted. After working corporate jobs that she did not enjoy, she decided it was time to stop settling for something that didn't make her happy and she chose to give child care a try. She loved it. Ella worked with multiple families and a day care facility. After working with a very special family, Ella received a job offer that she was not able to pass up. With her departure, she wanted to give the children a book to have as a keepsake. She searched for a short picture book with a child-care focus. The options were minimal. Naturally, as a 24-year-old graduate not sure where her life was headed, she thought, "Hey! I want this book, why don't I write it myself?" So, she did. Ella reached out to Elle, who is not only one of Ella's high school peers, but also a very good friend, and pitched her idea. With a lot of work, the two created Ella and Ellie LLC. and "Always Nanny."

Ella resides in Wisconsin and works at a local radio station as an on-air personality. She lives with her partner in life, Daniel. They enjoy spending time with their families, hiking, camping, and the occasional lazy night watching movies and indulging on pizza. Ella remains very close to the family that this story is based on.

About the Illustrator

As a child, Elle began drawing on the walls with crayon... and never really stopped. Elle is an American published Writer and Illustrator. For seven months in 2017 she traveled and worked within the film industry in Vancouver, Canada. She graduated from The Savannah College of Art and Design (SCAD) in 2014 with a BFA in 2D/3D Animation, where she learned to work by the saying Sleep Comes After Death. She is an experienced Animator/Designer with a demonstrated history of working in the marketing, editorial, fashion, and film industries. Elle is a professional skilled in illustration, typography, book/toy design, and production.

She is the co-founder of author and illustrator partnership Ella & Ellie LLC. with good friend and on-air personality Ella D. Elle has been a member of The Society of Children's Book Writers and Illustrators (SCBWI) since 2013. To get to know her main audience on a personal level, she has volunteered as an Art Therapist at her local hospital drawing with children. Her jewelry collection and series of miniature paintings have been shown in the Gutstein Gallery twice, Local Color Gallery, and sold in ShopSCAD.

In her spare time she enjoys dancing, traveling, and writing. You can check out more of her work at: www.ellebleycreative.com

® Ella & Ellie LLC.

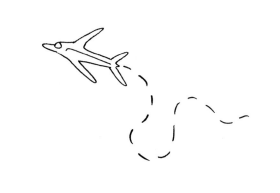

There are many ways to raise a family.
Sometimes a special addition, a nanny, can
make all the difference.

She is always there for you.
She always loves you.
She is always nanny.

Thank you
for all the
love & support!
Enjoy the book...
EB

Emily, thank you
so much for buying our book!
~ Ella D.

64225182R00018

Made in the USA
Middletown, DE
15 February 2018